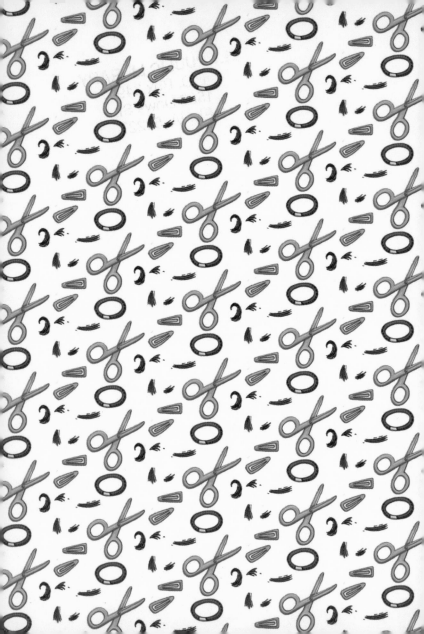

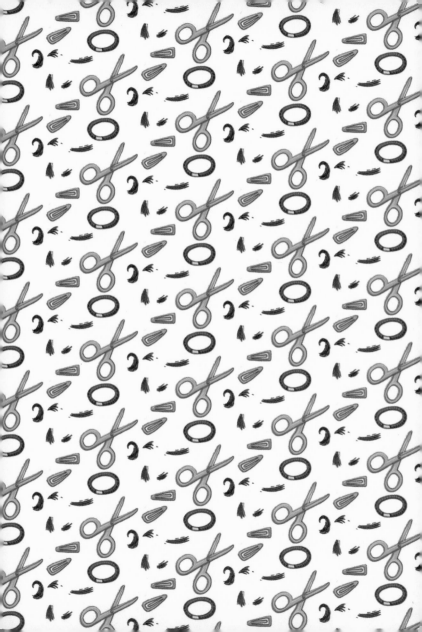

# Mary's HAIR

## Eoin Colfer

With illustrations by
Richard Watson

Barrington Stoke

First published in 2013 in Great Britain by
Barrington Stoke Ltd
18 Walker Street, Edinburgh, EH3 7LP

www.barringtonstoke.co.uk

This edition first published 2015

This story was first published in a different form in
*Kids' Night In* (Harper Collins, 2003)

Text © 2003 Eoin Colfer
Illustrations © 2013 Richard Watson

A CIP catalogue record for this book is available
from the British Library upon request

ISBN: 978-1-78112-510-6

Printed in China by Leo

This book has dyslexia friendly features

For anyone who has ever
had a bad hair day

# Contents

# Chapter 1

I hate my hair. Mammy says you mustn't hate anything, but I can't help it. I hate my hair!

Just look at it! It's all bits. Brown bits, black bits, curly bits and straight bits.

It looks like a big bush growing on top of my head. It would be no surprise if I woke up one spring morning to find a family of swallows nesting in my bushy hair.

It's not fair. Other girls have lovely blonde hair. The kind you can put into pigtails.

I tried to put my horrid hair into pigtails once. The elastic bobbles snapped in the middle of playtime. My hair popped out, more bushy than ever. My best friend Imelda said it was like my head had exploded.

Daddy says that if you don't like something, then you should do something about it, not just whine at your parents when they're trying to have a cup of tea.

So, one day, I decided to do just that. I made up my mind to cut my hair until it looked the way I wanted it to.

Just like those girls in the magazines.

# Chapter 2

I collected all the things I needed, and made a little pile on my dressing table.

There were –

* scissors from the drawer in the kitchen

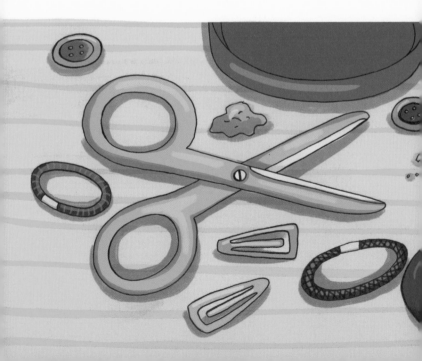

* a tub of my brother's hair gel to flatten the curly bits

* a pair of swim goggles to protect my eyes, in case the scissors slipped.

First I put on the hair gel.  It felt cold and slimy, like a family of snails crawling over my head.  At least it helped the goggles slide on smoothly.

Maybe I should have washed those goggles before I put them on.  There was all sorts of stuff inside.  Sand from the beach, a blob of chewing gum, and a dried-up old starfish.

Then it was time to cut. The scissors felt funny in my fingers. But there was no time to worry about that – Mammy could come in the door any second.

So, I set to work. I took it slow at first, just cutting one hair at a time. But when I saw how brilliant I was at hair-dressing, I started snipping as fast as I could.

Soon there were hundreds of curls on the bedroom carpet, like autumn leaves on the grass.

I took off the goggles. My hair looked brilliant. That was the last time the hair-dresser would get any money from me! I might open a hair-dresser's myself. In the bedroom.

'Mary's Hair,' I'd call it.

# Mary's Hair

## 10p a go

Bring your own goggles.

Nearly all my curls were gone now. There were just a few baby ones that I couldn't cut because the kitchen scissors were a bit blunt.

I gave myself a fringe, too. Very trendy. It was a little bit crooked, but you wouldn't see that if I walked around with my head to one side.

I didn't know why I was worried at all. Mammy wouldn't be one bit cross. In fact, she'd be pleased that I'd saved her some money.

# Chapter 3

It was time to try out my new hairdo.

All the girls would be playing at Imelda's. Saturday was Barbie Day and Imelda's daddy just got her the biggest Barbie house in the shop.

As I crept down the stairs, I made
sure to keep my head to one side
because of the fringe.

I don't know why I bothered creeping.
Mammy and Daddy were far too busy
trying to get baby Peter to open his
mouth for some porridge to notice
me. I don't blame Petey. I never liked
porridge either.

Imelda lived two doors down. On a normal day I'd go through a hole in the hedge. That day I went on the path, to protect my hairdo from any grabby branches.

Imelda's mammy, Gloria, was in the front window polishing a vase. I gave her a big wave, and pointed to my head. Gloria was so impressed that she dropped the vase. Who could blame her? She must have thought that I was one of those famous supermodels.

I could hear the girls round the back.
They were all going "ooh!" and "aah!"
and saying how great Imelda's doll's
house was.  Wait until they saw my hair!

I crept up behind the shrubs, then
hopped out right in front of the girls.

"Here I am, ladies!" I shouted. "What
do you think of me?"

# Chapter 4

No one said anything.  I don't think they knew who I was for a few seconds.  Then the best thing happened.  The girls started to clap.  A big clap, just for me.  You'd swear I was a pop star or something.  It was the happiest moment of my life.  I decided I'd better make a speech.

"You're too kind, girls," I said.  You'd think I was after winning an Oscar.  "I'd just like to thank my mother for buying the scissors.  And my big brother for leaving his door open, so I could borrow his hair gel.  And, of course, all my friends for giving me the guts to cut my own hair."

Imelda gave me a big hug, and a loan of Rollerblade Barbie.

Only Imelda's **best BEST** friend got
Rollerblade Barbie. We played for ages.
We played Barbie goes to school, Barbie
saves the ozone layer, and Barbie wins
the world boxing title. It was brilliant.

After a while, I noticed that the girls were looking at my head.

"Nice, isn't it?" I said. "It's hard to believe that it's all my own work."

Imelda shook her head. "It's not nice any more, Mary," she said. "The gel is dry now."

I reached up with my fingers. The curls were back. The gel felt different too. Not slimy any more. Hard as a helmet.

I got a funny feeling in my stomach. The kind you get just before a nasty shock. I dropped Rollerblade Barbie and picked up Imelda's mirror. The smile dropped off my face.

"Oh no," I said. My horrible bushy hair was back. Only now it was worse. My fringe had shrunk right up to the top of my forehead, and my curls looked like a million little horns.

# Chapter 5

Next thing I knew my mammy was standing in front of me. She'd come in for a gossip with Gloria, and spotted me in the garden.

"Mary!" she yelled. "What have you done?"

I wanted to blame someone else for a minute. But there was no one. Even Petey had been with Mam and Dad at the time.

"You cut your hair, didn't you?" Mam said.

I nodded. I was too scared to speak.

"Look at the state of you!" she said. "Well, I hope you've learned your lesson."

I nodded again. All the girls nodded along with me, just in case they were in trouble too.

"Get home now in front of me," Mam said. "Wait until your father sees this."

I started to cry then, big fat tears that dripped off the tip of my nose. It's a terrible thing to be popular for half an hour, and then have to go back to being plain old Mary Leary. I might never get a go of Rollerblade Barbie again.

I'd learned my lesson all right.

This is the lesson I'd learned –

If you're going to do something to your hair, it's a good idea to try it out on someone else first.

So I would have to find a volunteer for my hair experiments in future.

# Chapter 6

Mam made me promise never to cut my hair again. She even made sure that my fingers weren't crossed when I made the promise.

But she never said that I couldn't **dye** my hair.

So that was what I decided to do next. If my hair was a lovely blonde colour, you might not notice the crooked fringe and the spiky curls.

The next morning I went to look for a volunteer to test the dye on. I asked the girls, but they ran away screaming. That usually means no. So I had to ask someone who would do **anything** just to have a friend.

Noely Rochford always had a runny nose. By the age of seven he still hadn't figured out how to use a hanky.

This meant that not even the other boys wanted to hang around with him, and they were a fairly smelly bunch themselves. So when I called at Noely's house that Sunday, he was a bit surprised to see me.

Noely came to the door wearing a woolly hat, Pooh PJs and fuzzy bunny slippers.

"How would you like a friend?" I said.

"Who is it?" he asked.

"Me.  But only for today."

Noely thought about it for a second. He wiped his nose on his PJ sleeve.  "OK."

"There's one condition though. You'll have to get your hair dyed blond."

Noely wiped his nose on the other sleeve. "OK."

"Come on then," I said. "The hair-dresser's is in my house. I'll sit on the wall until you get changed."

"Changed?"

Boys!  They've no brains.

"You need to change into your clothes, Noely.  You can't wear your PJs through the estates."

"Oh.  OK."

It took Noely almost an hour to get changed. My bum was getting sore sitting on the wall. I was thinking about looking for another volunteer, when the door opened and out he came.

"Oh no!" I moaned. Noely had taken his hat off, and there was no hair on his head – only fuzz!

"I got a shave," he said. "A number two. Do you like it?"

"No, Noely, I don't like it," I said. "How am I supposed to dye a bald head?"

I thought Noely was going to cry then.

"Are you not my friend any more?"
he said.

I almost said no. But then I
remembered something.

"Noely. Don't you have a dog? A
little shaggy-haired dog?"

"Yep," said Noely. "Bruce is my best friend in the world."

"Hmm," I said. I had had another brilliant idea. "Why don't you ask him to come with us?"

# Chapter 7

My brilliant idea was to dye the dog's hair. If the whole thing went wrong, Bruce wouldn't even be able to complain, except to other dogs.

I sneaked Noely and Bruce upstairs to the bathroom.

There was no need to sneak, of course. Mammy and Daddy were busy trying to stop Petey kicking long enough to change his nappy.

Bruce was perfect for my practice run. He had a big head of shaggy brown hair. Almost exactly the same as mine. Now all I had to do was get Bruce into the shower. The steps on the packet of hair dye were simple –

1. Wet the hair.

2. Rub in the dye.

No problem.

I gave Noely his orders.

"Tell Bruce to get into the bath. You get in with him and hold his head still."

Noely sniffed. "Can't."

"And why not, Mister Rochford?" I said. The teacher always called Noely "Mister Rochford" when she was annoyed with him.

"I'm not allowed in the bath without my mammy, Teacher," Noely said. "I mean, Mary."

"Well how am I supposed to wet Bruce's hair then? And what's he doing now?"

Bruce had his head stuck down the toilet. His back legs were up on the toilet seat.

"He's having a drink," Noely said. "Bruce loves drinking out of the toilet."

And then I had another brilliant idea. I crept over to the toilet, and lifted off the cistern lid. It was really heavy, but I'm very strong for my size.

The water inside was blue, because of the toilet bleach, but I thought it should be OK to use. I poured in all the hair dye, and stirred it around with Daddy's toothbrush.

Then I flushed the toilet!

**Whoosh** went the water, all over Bruce's head. The poor dog fell right into the bowl, where he spun round and round with the blue water.

Noely started to cry. "Bruce is drowning! What have you done, Mary Leary?"

Maybe my idea wasn't so brilliant after all.

But then the toilet stopped flushing, and Bruce's head popped up over the rim.

"Ruff," said Bruce. It wasn't a happy "ruff". It was an I'll-get-you-for-that "ruff". He hopped out of the toilet and ran off down the stairs.

Noely ran off after his dog. I didn't understand why Bruce was so upset.

It was only a bit of hair dye and some bleach. Now I couldn't even check the results of the dye.

I was putting Daddy's toothbrush back when I spotted something odd. All the bristles were gone. They had melted away. Now what could have done that?

# Chapter 8

Mammy made me go and say sorry to Noely. He was still crying even after two days.

"Sorry, Noely," I said. I tried to sound really sad.

"You made Bruce all funny-looking, Mary Leary."

It was true. Bruce did look funny. Half his body was white, and the other half was brown. He looked like two dogs stuck together.

"I think he looks nice," I said. "Like a superhero dog."

"Really?"

"Really. Do you forgive me now?"

"No.  And Bruce doesn't either."

That was a surprise.  I thought Noely would forgive me straight away, just so he would have a friend.

"Friends forgive each other," I said.

Noely lifted his sleeve to wipe his
nose.  There was a plaster on the sleeve.
There was a message written on the
plaster.  It said, "Use your hanky."  Noely
took a hanky from his pocket and gave
his nose a big blow.

"You're not my real friend," he said.
"You only wanted to play so you could
turn Bruce white.  Bruce is my real
friend."

Noely was right.  Bruce was his real friend.  I'd only called at his house because none of the girls would let me dye their hair.

"If I play with you for a week, will you forgive me then?" I asked.

Noely thought about it.  "A month."

"Two weeks."

"OK," he said.  "It's a deal."

We shook hands, because that's what you do when you make a deal.  Noely's hand was a bit sticky.  I heard Mammy calling me from up the street.

"I have to go now," I said.

"Where?"

"Mammy's taking me to have my hair cut short, so it'll grow out all the same length."

"You're getting a skinner?" Noely asked.

I nodded.  I didn't want a skinner.  I hadn't had short hair since I was a baby.

Noely smiled.  "Well don't worry, Mary.  Even if your hair turns out horrible, I'll still play with you."

"Thanks, Noely. You're a real friend."

I ran up the road. Mammy was beeping the car horn for me to hurry up.

Maybe Noely wouldn't be such a bad friend after all. He had a cool dog, and he was good at taking orders. The most important thing was that he was learning to use a hanky.

No more tricks.  Real friends didn't play tricks.

Anyway, Mammy had banned me from using hair dye.  So now I couldn't cut or dye my hair.

But Mammy hadn't said anything about perms.

Maybe I could give myself one of those.

Our books are tested
for children and young people by
children and young people.

Thanks to everyone who consulted on
a manuscript for their time and effort in
helping us to make our books better
for our readers.

# Have you read all the Little Gems?

# New!
# COLOUR
# Little Gems

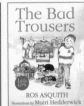